Do Little Mermaids Wet Their Beds?

Story by Jeanne Willis
Pictures by Penelope Jossen

Albert Whitman & Company
Morton Grove, Illinois

For Sylvie — J. W.
For all little mermaids — P. J.

Library of Congress Cataloging-in-Publication Data

Willis, Jeanne.

Do little mermaids wet their beds? / story by Jeanne Willis; pictures

by Penelope Jossen.

p. cm.

Summary: Cecelia meets a mermaid who assures her that her

bedwetting problem will soon be solved.

ISBN 0-8075-1668-6 (hardcover)

[1. Bedwetting—Fiction. 2. Mermaids—Fiction. 3. Stories in rhyme.]

I. Jossen, Penelope, ill. II. Title.

PZ8.3.W6799 Do 2001

[E]—dc21

00-010203

I knew a lovely little girl,
I think that she was four.
And yet she was as clever
as a five-year-old, or more!

She washed herself

and dressed herself,

and used a knife and fork.

She could dial a real telephone
and answer it and talk.

She could ride her brother's bicycle,

and write her name in pen.

And did she lose the pen caps?
No! She put them on again.

She'd given up her stroller;
she preferred to walk instead—

but I hate to have to tell you this,
she always wet the bed.

She didn't mean to do it!
But no matter how she tried,
there were stains on certain mattresses
and sheets hung up outside.

There were lots of soggy nighties
and some matching underwear—
and guess what else went in the wash?
Her favorite teddy bear!

She didn't drink much at bedtime
and she tried and tried again
to go before she went to sleep—
but nothing happened *then*.

Mom said, "One day
you'll wake up dry—
it just takes time, my sweet."
But she lay in bed and worried
on a horrid plastic sheet.

At last one night, she had a dream
that, far away at sea,
she heard a little mermaid
calling, "Come and play with me."

And so she packed a suitcase
with her most important things:
her ballet shoes, tiara,
and a pair of fairy wings.

She found a piece of paper
and she wrote a little note.
"I have run away to sea," it said.
She got her hat and coat.

She found her rabbit slippers,
and she put them
on her feet…

and dreamt she tiptoed down the stairs,
and skipped off down the street.

Did she meet the mermaid?
Yes, I'm glad to say!
They rode upon a seahorse…

and some dolphins came to play.

They had a sing-song with some whales;
the oysters gave them pearls.

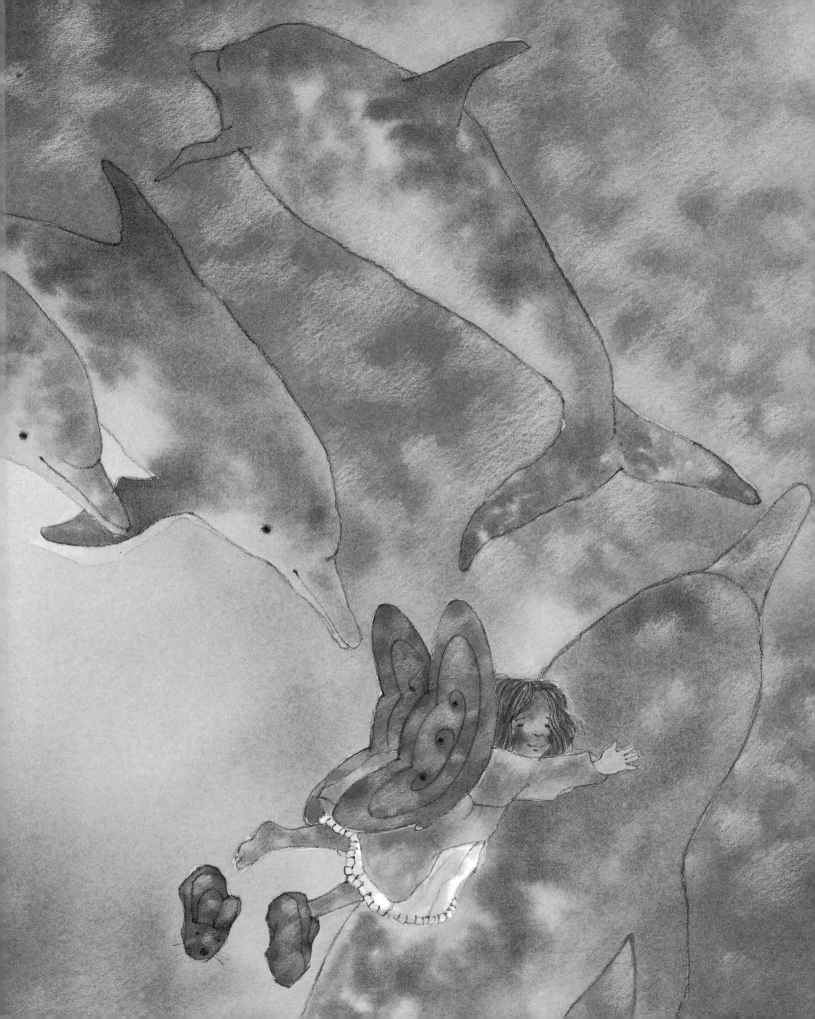

They danced 'til dawn with tiger prawns—
such very tired girls!

They lay down on the seabed
on a mattress made of sand,
and our little girl was happy
for the mermaid held her hand.

She said, "I used to wet *my* bed.
It didn't worry me!
What does a little puddle matter
in the mighty sea?
You'll soon stay dry all night;
'til then you're not alone.
I'm sure when she was four
the Queen of England wet her throne."

All in a dream they waved goodbye.

The little girl ran home…

and crept upstairs, her hair all wet,
her slippers dripping foam.

She slid between her own clean sheets,
and when the morning came…

she felt her mother kissing her
and calling out her name:

"Cecelia, your coat is soaked!
Your hat is wet! But why,
Cecelia! You clever girl—
your bed is nice and dry!"

Wetting the bed is a normal part of a child's development, and it will usually cease by the end of the toddler years. Parents can help by encouraging their child to urinate and defecate before sleep, and realizing that little children who fall asleep "dead tired" after an overly busy day may bedwet. It is not recommended that fluids be greatly restricted before bedtime.

Sometimes the process may be helped by simply raising a child's awareness of bedwetting. This can be done by talking about bedwetting, reading stories such as *Do Little Mermaids Wet Their Beds?,* or encouraging your child to draw pictures.(You might say, "Draw a picture of yourself sleeping in bed. Now draw a picture of yourself walking to the toilet at night.")

Children over five years old, adolescents, and even adults who still wet the bed can benefit from a medically based program that will evaluate the cause of wetting and initiate a treatment plan.

Max Maizels, M.D., Pediatric Urologist
Director, Program in Pediatric Enurology
TRY for DRY Clinic, Children's Memorial Hospital, Chicago, Illinois
Professor of Urology, Northwestern University Medical School